Eve's Green Garden

The Sound of Long E

by Cecilia Minden and Joanne Meier · illustrated by Bob Ostrom

The Child's World

Published by The Child's World®
1980 Lookout Drive
Mankato, MN 56003-1705
800-599-READ
www.childsworld.com

The Child's World®: Mary Berendes, Publishing Director
The Design Lab: Design and page production
Richard Carbajal: Color

Library of Congress Cataloging-in-Publication Data
Minden, Cecilia.
  Eve's green garden : the sound of long e / by Cecilia
Minden and Joanne Meier ; illustrated by Bob Ostrom.
    p. cm.
  ISBN 978-1-60253-399-8 (library bound : alk. paper)
  1. English language—Vowels—Juvenile literature. 2.
English language—Phonetics—Juvenile literature 3.
Reading—Phonetic method—Juvenile literature. I. Meier,
Joanne D. II. Ostrom, Bob. III. Title.
  PE1157.M564 2010
  [E]—dc22   2010002911

Printed in the United States of America in Mankato, MN.
July 2010
F11538

NOTE TO PARENTS AND EDUCATORS:

The Child's World® has created this series with the goal of exposing children to engaging stories and illustrations that assist in phonics development. The books in the series will help children learn the relationships between the letters of written language and the individual sounds of spoken language. This contact helps children learn to use these relationships to read and write words.

The books in this series follow a similar format. An introductory page, to be read by an adult, introduces the child to the phonics feature, or sound, that will be highlighted in the book. Read this page to the child, stressing the phonic feature. Help the student learn how to form the sound with her mouth. The story and engaging illustrations follow the introduction. At the end of the story, word lists categorize the feature words into their phonic elements.

Each book in this series has been carefully written to meet specific readability requirements. Close attention has been paid to elements such as word count, sentence length, and vocabulary. Readability formulas measure the ease with which the text can be read and understood. Each book in this series has been analyzed using the Spache readability formula.

Reading research suggests that systematic phonics instruction can greatly improve students' word recognition, spelling, and comprehension skills. This series assists in the teaching of phonics by providing students with important opportunities to apply their knowledge of phonics as they read words, sentences, and text.

The letter e makes two sounds.

The short sound of **e** sounds like **e** as in: *egg* and *hen*.

The long sound of **e** sounds like **e** as in: *bee* and *heel*.

In this book, you will read words that have the long **e** sound as in: *deep, seeds, feeds,* and *weeds.*

Eve is planting a garden.

She will grow vegetables.

Eve makes three rows.

She digs deep holes.

Eve puts seeds in the holes.

She covers the seeds with dirt.

The seeds will sleep in the earth. Seeds need time to grow.

Eve feeds the seeds plant food. Seeds need food to grow.

Eve waters the seeds.

Seeds need water to grow.

Soon the plants are growing.

Eve can see green plants.

Eve gets on her knees.

She needs to pull weeds.

Weeds keep plants

from growing.

Eve likes to be in the garden. She likes to see green plants grow.

Fun Facts

You might think that all seeds are tiny enough to fit inside the palm of your hand. This isn't true, however, for the seed of the double coconut palm tree. This seed can take 10 years to develop and has weighed in at more than 44 pounds (20 kilograms)! Double coconut palm trees are located on a chain of islands in the Indian Ocean.

Most people think weeds are annoying and try to keep them out of their gardens, but certain weeds can also be useful! Dandelions are a well-known weed. But, dandelion leaves are often used in salads, and the roots are sometimes an ingredient in a drink that is similar to coffee.

Activity

Planting Seeds in Your Garden

If you think you might make a good gardener, ask your parents if you can plant your own small garden in the backyard. Discuss what kinds of seeds you want to use and what time of year it is best to plant them. Once you have planted your seeds, be sure to water the garden regularly. Also pull any weeds that you see sprouting nearby. Keep a journal with pictures and notes describing how your plants are growing.

To Learn More

Books
About the Sound of Long E
Moncure, Jane Belk. *My "e" Sound Box®*. Mankato, MN: The Child's World, 2009.

About Green Plants
Berenstain, Stan, and Jan Berenstain. *The Berenstain Bears Grow-It! Mother Nature Has Such a Green Thumb!* New York: Random House, 1996.

Wade, Mary Dodson. *People Need Plants!* Berkeley Heights, NJ: Enslow Elementary, 2009.

About Seeds
Jordan, Helene J., and Loretta Krupinski (illustrator). *How a Seed Grows*. New York: HarperCollins Publishers, 1992.

Richard, Jean, and Anca Hariton (illustrator). *A Fruit Is a Suitcase for Seeds*. Minneapolis, MN: First Avenue Editions, 2006.

About Weeds
Wade, Mary Dodson. *Trees, Weeds, and Vegetables—So Many Kinds of Plants!* Berkeley Heights, NJ: Enslow Elementary, 2009.

Web Sites
Visit our home page for lots of links about the Sound of Long E:

childsworld.com/links

Note to Parents, Teachers, and Librarians: We routinely check our Web links to make sure they're safe, active sites—so encourage your readers to check them out!

Long E
Feature Words

Proper Names
Eve

Feature Words in Medial Position
deep
feeds
keep
need
seed
weeds

Feature Word in Final Position
be
knee
see
she

Feature Words with Blends and Digraphs
green
sleep
three

About the Authors

Cecilia Minden, PhD, is the former director of the Language and Literacy Program at the Harvard Graduate School of Education. She is now a reading consultant for school and library publications. She earned her PhD in reading education from the University of Virginia. Cecilia and her husband, Dave Cupp, live outside Chapel Hill, North Carolina. They enjoy sharing their love of reading with their grandchildren, Chelsea and Qadir.

Joanne Meier, PhD, has worked as an elementary school teacher, university professor, and researcher. She earned her BA in early childhood education from the University of South Carolina, and her MEd and PhD in education from the University of Virginia. She currently works as a literacy consultant for schools and private organizations. Joanne lives in Virginia with her husband Eric, daughters Kella and Erin, two cats, and a gerbil.

About the Illustrator

Bob Ostrom has been illustrating children's books for nearly twenty years. A graduate of the New England School of Art & Design at Suffolk University, Bob has worked for such companies as Disney, Nickelodeon, and Cartoon Network. He lives in North Carolina with his wife Melissa and three children, Will, Charlie, and Mae.